P9-DMU-758

To Nick Meglin, Tom Gammill, and all sorts of new friends

Printed in Singapore
Reinforced binding

First Edition, June 2014
10 9 8 7 6 5 4
F850-6835-5-15009

Library of Congress Cataloging-in-Publication Data

Willems, Mo.
 My new friend is so fun! / by Mo Willems. — 1st ed.
   p. cm.
 "An Elephant & Piggie Book."
 Summary: Gerald the elephant and Snake fear that Piggie and Brian Bat will have so much fun together they will no longer need their best friends.
 ISBN 978-1-4231-7958-0
[1. Best friends—Fiction. 2. Friendship—Fiction. 3. Animals—Fiction. 4. Humorous stories.] I. Title.
 PZ7.W65535Myn 2013
 [E]—dc23   2012022223

Visit www.hyperionbooksforchildren.com
and www.pigeonpresents.com

An ELEPHANT & PIGGIE Book

Hyperion Books for Children

New York

AN IMPRINT OF DISNEY BOOK GROUP

My New Friend Is So Fun!

By **Mo Willems**

Hi, Gerald!

4

Fun!

Brian Bat is nice!

They must be having
a *super* fun time!

Yeah!

19

23

24

25

Brian!

31

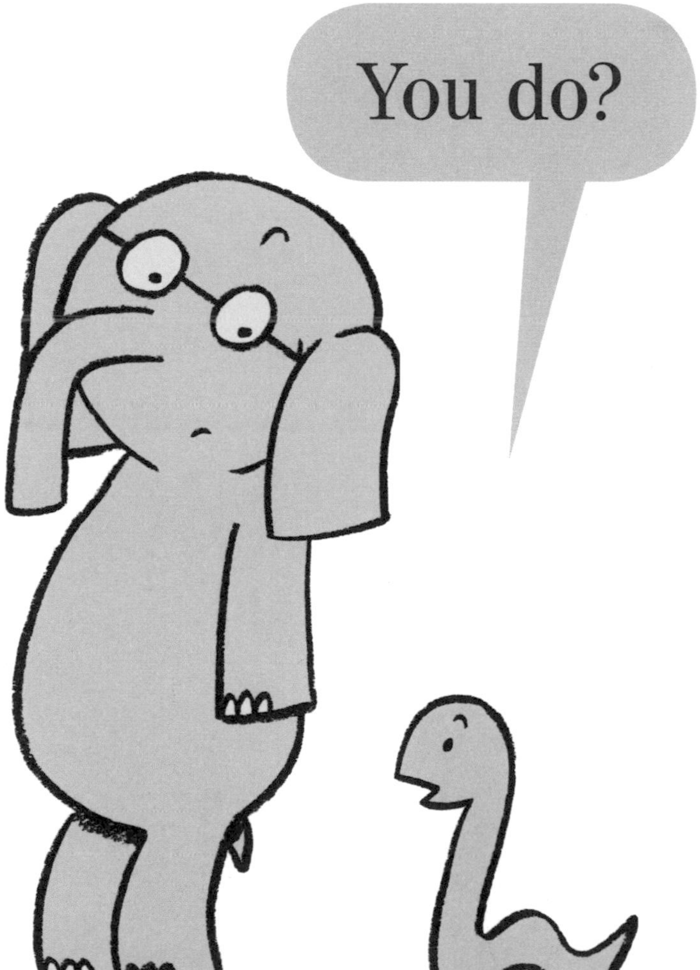
You do?

Best Friend games?

It's Best Friend fun!

44

45

Do you want
to see our
drawings?

47

49

Of course!

You are *our* Best Friends.

Elephant and Piggie have more funny adventures in:

Today I Will Fly!

My Friend Is Sad

I Am Invited to a Party!

There Is a Bird on Your Head!
(Theodor Seuss Geisel Medal)

I Love My New Toy!

I Will Surprise My Friend!

Are You Ready to Play Outside?
(Theodor Seuss Geisel Medal)

Watch Me Throw the Ball!

Elephants Cannot Dance!

Pigs Make Me Sneeze!

I Am Going!

Can I Play Too?

We Are in a Book!
(Theodor Seuss Geisel Honor)

I Broke My Trunk!
(Theodor Seuss Geisel Honor)

Should I Share My Ice Cream?

Happy Pig Day!

Listen to My Trumpet!

Let's Go for a Drive!
(Theodor Seuss Geisel Honor)

A Big Guy Took My Ball!
(Theodor Seuss Geisel Honor)

I'm a Frog!

Waiting Is Not Easy!